Turtle Dreams

The Story of I Can't
Copyright © 2006 Turtle Dreams.
www.turtledreams.co.uk

First Published in Great Britain 2006
by Turtle Dreams

First Edition

An original concept by Robert Page.
Text Copyright © 2006 Robert Page.
Illustrations Copyright © 2006 Julie Fisher.

ISBN 0-9554205-0-4
ISBN 978-0-9554205-0-4

Printed and bound in Great Britain by
Aldine Print Ltd, Great Malvern

The Story of

Written by
Robert Page

Illustrated by
Julie Fisher

Once upon a time there were two friends called I Can and I Can't.

They looked alike.

They sounded alike.

They both felt soft, squidgy and warm to touch.

Despite the fact that they were both so similar they had very different lives.

I Can did lots of things.

I Can't didn't do much.

I Can was often
excited.

I Can't was always worried.

I Can Knew lots of people.

I Can't didn't.

They both knew someone called Opportunity who would regularly knock on their doors and invite them out.

"OK!" I Can would say and off they would go to have adventures.

I Can't would just stay in with a friend called Fear.

Everyday Opportunity and I Can would go out and I Can't would stay in with Fear.

But I Can't felt safe
with Fear and after a
while Opportunity
stopped calling.

One day I Can asked
I Can't a question.

"Why don't you ever come on adventures with me and Opportunity?"

"I want to," says I Can't.

"So, why don't you?" says I Can.

"My friend, Fear, always seems to get in my way and stop me," says I Can't.

"Huh! Some friend," says I Can, "to stop you from having fun with us."

"Fear is only trying to protect me," says I Can't.

"Fear is a friend of mine too and protects me but is far too small to ever get in my way," says I Can.

"That's strange," says
I Can't, "Fear seems
quite big to me.
What can I do?"

"Simple!" says I Can, "Ask
Fear to step aside and
let you do something."

Eventually, I Can't became bored staying in with Fear, so asked, very politely, if Fear would step aside and let Opportunity in.

To the amazement of
I Can't, Fear said "Sure!"
and stepped aside. Then
there was a knock at
the door.

It was I Can and Opportunity, who said, "Hello. Would you like to come on an adventure with us?".

"Yes, please," said I Can't with a rather large smile.

The three of them had
so much fun and did so
many things together
that day.

When I Can't returned home, Fear was waiting and although it seemed strange, I Can't was certain that Fear had shrunk a little.

I Can't spent more and more time with I Can and Opportunity and had more and more fun.

After a while, I Can't felt like a new person and decided to have a new name... I Can Too.

Once upon a time there were two friends called I Can and I Can Too.

And they did everything together.

The End.

over to you